Raymond and Graham

RULE the SCHOOL

Raymond and Graham
RULE the SCHOOL

by **Mike Knudson**
and **Steve Wilkinson**
Illustrated by **Stacy Curtis**

VIKING

VIKING
Published by Penguin Group
Penguin Young Readers Group, 345 Hudson Street, New York, New York 10014, U.S.A.
Penguin Group (Canada), 90 Eglinton Avenue East, Suite 700, Toronto, Ontario, Canada M4P 2Y3
(a division of Pearson Penguin Canada Inc.)
Penguin Books Ltd, 80 Strand, London WC2R 0RL, England
Penguin Ireland, 25 St Stephen's Green, Dublin 2, Ireland (a division of Penguin Books Ltd)
Penguin Group (Australia), 250 Camberwell Road, Camberwell, Victoria 3124, Australia
(a division of Pearson Australia Group Pty Ltd)
Penguin Books India Pvt Ltd, 11 Community Centre, Panchsheel Park, New Delhi—110 017, India
Penguin Group (NZ), 67 Apollo Drive, Rosedale, North Shore 0632, New Zealand
Penguin Books (South Africa) (Pty) Ltd, 24 Sturdee Avenue, Rosebank, Johannesburg 2196, South Africa

Penguin Books Ltd, Registered Offices: 80 Strand, London WC2R 0RL, England

First published in a slightly different form by Banjo Books, 2005
This edition published by Viking, a division of Penguin Young Readers Group, 2008

5 7 9 10 8 6 4

Text copyright © Mike Knudson and Steve Wilkinson, 2005, 2008
Illustrations copyright © Stacy Curtis, 2008
All rights reserved

LIBRARY OF CONGRESS CATALOGING-IN-PUBLICATION DATA
Knudson, Mike.
Raymond and Graham rule the school / by Mike Knudson and Steve Wilkinson ; illustrations by Stacy Curtis.
p. cm.
Summary: Best friends Raymond and Graham have looked forward to being the "oldest, coolest, toughest"
boys at East Millcreek Elementary School, but from the start of fourth grade everything goes wrong, from
getting the scary teacher to not getting the lead in the school play.
ISBN 978-0-670-01101-8 (hardcover)
[1. Elementary schools—Fiction. 2. Schools—Fiction. 3. Theater—Fiction. 4. Self-confidence—Fiction.
5. Best friends—Fiction. 6. Friendship—Fiction.] I. Wilkinson, Steve. II. Curtis, Stacy, ill. III. Title.
PZ7.K7836Ray 2008
[Fic]—dc22
2007033350

Manufactured in China   Set in Chaparral MM   Book design by Jim Hoover

To our East Millcreek Elementary
classmates and to the memory of mean
old Mrs. Gibson, the best teacher
we ever had.   —M.K and S.W.

For Levi   —S.C.

Prologue

IT WAS THE end of summer vacation. Every kid in the world was dreading the unavoidable return to school. And if it were any other year, Graham and I would be miserable, too.

But not this year, no siree! This would be different. It would be a year to remember, a year like no other, a year we would look back on eighty years from now when we were old and wrinkly and say to ourselves, "That was the best year ever!" Yes, it was finally here. *Fourth grade!* That's right, FOURTH GRADE! We were no longer little kids. We would be the oldest, coolest, toughest kids at East Millcreek Elementary. Oh, yes! This would be the year we would RULE THE SCHOOL!

1

Fourth-Grade Men

NINE O'CLOCK in the morning and it was already hot. I was shooting hoops with Graham on his driveway, discussing our soon-to-be fourth-grade kingdom. We've been best friends forever, since we were little kids. Graham is still pretty short. The coolest thing about Graham is that he has red hair and about a million freckles. We tried to count them once, but we got tired after just counting the freckles on one of his hands.

We were excited for school to start, and it was only two days away. The first day was on a Wednesday this year. So not only did we get to start fourth grade, but we also got to have a short week of school.

I stopped dribbling and tried to spin the ball on my finger.

"Hey, Graham, remember Gordon Armstrong?" I asked. The ball wobbled on my finger for a moment and then fell off.

"Of course I remember Gordon Armstrong," Graham said, smiling.

We must have had this same conversation a hundred times that summer. But somehow it never seemed to get old. Gordon Armstrong was in fourth grade when we were in first grade, and without question, he ruled the school back then. Everything about Gordon was cool. The way he walked, the way he talked . . . everything. And he was huge, almost twice as big as me or Graham. We knew he was The King the first moment we saw him. He was strutting down the hall with Michelle Johnson, the prettiest girl at East Millcreek Elementary. As they passed by, we immediately jumped aside like we were microwave popcorn or something. Gordon looked down at us and with half a smile simply said, "Hi, boys."

I know it doesn't sound like much, but we understood him loud and clear. He really meant, "Hey, look at me, I'm a fourth-grade *man* holding hands with a good-looking fourth-grade *lady*, and you two are just a couple of puny little boys." And he was right. We hated the fact that he could be so right. Gordon was a man. He had real muscles and everything. And us, well, we were just puny little kids with absolutely no muscles at all.

Yes, ever since that day, Graham and I had waited and waited for our day to come. The day we would become FOURTH-GRADE MEN. The day we would become Gordon Armstrong. We were ready to give a simple "Hi, boys" to some poor, tiny first-grade boys and have them look up at us in awe.

"Yeah, Gordon was cool," Graham said. "But doesn't it seem like he was a lot taller than we are now? I still feel kinda small."

"Yeah, I was thinking the same thing. Plus, Michelle Johnson looked a lot different from the girls our age. She seemed more, you know, womanly or something," I said, passing him the ball.

"Oh, well, we're still going to rule the school!" Graham said.

Everything seemed perfect. The only thing that could possibly go wrong would be to get stuck in Mrs. Gibson's class. I got the shivers just thinking her name. Mrs. Gibson is about a hundred years old. To simply say she's scary would be too kind. She's much worse than scary. She's almost like some kind of tall, wrinkly, old, creepy, monsterish being from a horror movie.

Even back in first grade I had heard stories about old Mrs. Gibson. But I didn't experience her evil firsthand until I reached second grade. I remember it like it was yesterday. There I was, standing in the lunch line, minding my own business, when something cold and bony touched the back of my neck. Whatever it was somehow drained the blood from my neck and sent it down my spine like ice water. At the same time, I heard an old, raspy voice say, "Excuse me." My stomach leaped to my throat as I slowly turned to see what was on my neck. I looked up into old Mrs. Gibson's squinty eyes staring down at me through these huge glasses. Without thinking, I screamed like I'd never screamed before and ran down the hall waving my hands in all directions like a maniac. I didn't turn back until I was safely outside on the playground.

I didn't dare return to the lunchroom for fear she would still be there, so I sat outside, hungry as could be, waiting for everyone else to finish lunch and come out to play. Some kids came out and made fun of me. But I didn't care. At least I was still alive.

As long as I didn't get stuck in her class, life would be good. But it didn't worry me too much, because ever since kindergarten, I've always had the best teachers. It's like I've had some kind of good-teacher luck throughout my whole elementary-school life. I worried about Graham, though. He always seemed to get the bad ones. Like in second grade, I had Mrs. Bigler. We played kickball for P.E. and fun stuff like that. Graham, on the other hand, had Mrs. Jones. For P.E., their class would do weird things like learn pioneer dances. Mrs. Jones looked old, too. I'll bet she was at least ninety. Who knows, maybe she was even a pioneer once. I mean, why else would you do pioneer dancing for P.E.? It's not a sport, a game, or even fun. Plus, pioneers aren't around anymore, so why would you ever need to dance like them?

Anyway, we only had one more day before we found out who our teachers would be. Tomorrow morning, the class assignments would be posted on the school doors.

I stole the basketball from Graham and threw up one last shot.

"Air ball!" he laughed, as my shot missed the rim by about a mile.

2

Mrs. Gibson

THE NEXT DAY, I got up early and walked down to school with Graham. Every year the new class lists were taped on the front doors the day before school started. Usually we just waited for the first day of school to find out who our teachers were. But this year, we had to know the very moment the lists were posted. On our way, we talked again about Gordon Armstrong. We wondered what he must look like now, as a seventh-grader. We especially wondered what Michelle Johnson looked like. After a lot of wondering, we finally arrived at the school grounds.

There was already a bunch of kids looking at the

lists. Graham and I stopped and looked at each other. Then, at the same time, we took a deep breath and slowly walked up the school steps to the lists on the front doors. I said a little prayer in my head that I wouldn't be listed in that creepy old woman's class. I scanned the class lists and immediately found Mrs. Gibson's name. *Please don't be in her class, please don't be in her class,* I chanted in my mind as I read down the list. Unfortunately, it took me less than one second to zero in on my name. I closed my eyes and shook my head.

"It can't be," I said. Maybe I didn't really see what I thought I saw. Slowly, I opened my eyes again. My heart was pounding, and I started breathing faster and faster. No! Oh, no! There it was as big as life! "Raymond Knudson" right in the middle of Mrs. Gibson's class list. It seemed to be twice the size of the other names. Suddenly I felt all shaky and queasy, like I was about to puke. I buried my head in my hands. *This can't be happening,* I thought. This was the year I was supposed to rule the school! The year I had waited for since the first grade. I was supposed to be Gordon Armstrong!

Maybe my mom would send a note to the school saying I'm allergic to old, tall, skinny, evil women with squinty eyes, or something like that. As I was concocting lies in my head to get out of Mrs. Gibson's class, Graham spoke up and broke my concentration.

"It won't be so bad," he said. "Look, I'm in there, too. We can be miserable together. It'll be fun."

I looked over at Graham like he was out of his mind. I couldn't believe what he just said.

"Oh, so it won't be that bad?" I said with a fake smile. "You think it'll be fun, do you?" Then, without even thinking, I blurted out, "That's easy for *you to say*!" My voice came out louder and louder with every word. "You always get bad teachers! No offense, but you must be used to it! I always have good teachers! And now, when it counts, when it really, really counts, my *fourth-grade year*, I get stuck with the oldest, creepiest teacher on earth!" I was so mad I didn't know what to do. As I turned around to walk down the stairs, I bumped into a tall, thin pole.

"Great!" I screamed. "Not only do I get the worst teacher on earth but then I bump into—" I couldn't even finish my sentence. That pole I bumped into wasn't a pole at all—it was a person. I slowly looked up in horror as I saw Mrs. Gibson staring down at me. I felt that same urge to run away screaming like a madman, but somehow I couldn't move. It was like those squinty little eyes had some kind of supernatural freezing power over me.

Mrs. Gibson didn't move, either. She must have been thinking of how she was going to kill me. Would it be a slow death, torturing me little by little each day throughout the school year, or would she just get it over with right now in front of all these kids? Finally she made her move.

"Excuse me, young man. Are you all right?" she said.

I tried to nod my head, but I was so scared I couldn't move it up or down. In fact, I couldn't move anything—my arms, my legs, nothing. Then I swear she made what almost looked like a smile with her wrinkly mouth and walked into the school.

I stared at her as she disappeared through the door. After a minute or two, I began to breathe again. Then, slowly, my arms and legs got their strength back.

"What just happened?" I asked Graham in a shaky voice.

"Well, you just screamed out loud that you have the worst teacher on earth while that teacher was standing right in back of you. Then you bumped into her. Then you just stood there like an idiot. Then she went inside the school. Then you asked me what happened. And then . . . well, you know the rest," Graham said.

"That's what I was afraid of. I was hoping it was just a bad dream," I said, still feeling a little weak. "I wonder what she's going to do to me."

"She seemed nice," Graham said. "Didn't you see that thing she did with her mouth? I think it was supposed to be a smile. I don't think she'll do anything to you."

"Are you *crazy*? Of course she's going to do something! This is Mrs. Gibson we're talking about,"

I reminded him. "Remember when Nick Peterson was in her class? The day after Mrs. Gibson made him stay after school in detention, he disappeared forever."

"I thought Nick's family moved to Chicago," Graham said, looking confused.

"Sure, that's what they say. But who knows what really happened?"

We left as fast as we could, before Mrs. Gibson came back outside. I calmed down about halfway home.

"I'm sorry I yelled at you, Graham. I didn't mean it. I was just, you know, freaked out about the list. I wonder if she heard me. Do you think she heard me? Maybe she didn't even hear me," I said, talking quickly and starting to get nervous again. "Or maybe she'll just forget about it by tomorrow. I mean . . . she's old. Old people always forget stuff, right? Yeah. Maybe, just maybe, I'll survive after all."

"Yeah," Graham answered, putting his hand on my shoulder. "I'm sure it will be fine."

I hoped he was right.

3

The Tradition Continues

THE NEXT MORNING, Graham and I walked to school again for the official first day of the year. I was still scared about the whole bumping-into-Mrs.-Gibson episode, but hey—maybe she'd forgotten about it.

We got to school early so we could have some time to roam the halls and look over our new kingdom. And you know what? It felt pretty good. We were officially LARGE and IN CHARGE! Graham and I turned the corner by the office and saw some puny first-grade boys standing by the drinking fountain. We paused and smiled at each other like a reflection in a mirror. The moment had arrived at last. The moment we'd thought about since first grade.

"This is it, Raymond. We've been waiting a long time for this moment—would you like the honors?" Graham asked.

"Be my guest, Mr. Fourth-Grade *Man*," I said, patting him on the shoulder.

Immediately our walks turned to struts. As we passed by, Graham turned on his coolest fourth-grade voice and said, "Hi, boys."

Their reply was just as we'd dreamed it would be all these years! Sure, Graham was walking down the hall with me instead of a girl like Michelle Johnson, but the effect was still the same. The little first-graders couldn't even talk. One of them raised his tiny hand and gave us a jittery wave, like he couldn't believe someone of our greatness could possibly be talking to him.

"Poor guy," Graham said, "he'll be thinking of me every day from now until the day he starts fourth grade. The day he'll become not Gordon Armstrong but Graham Wilkinson."

It felt like we were we carrying on some time-honored tradition, a tradition passed down from fourth-graders to first-graders every first day of school since the beginning of time. I imagined a fourth-grade caveman strutting down the stone hall in a cave school, giving a small cave boy a smile and a friendly "Ooga" as he passed by. I pictured that cave boy looking forward to the day he would become a big, hairy, stinky fourth-grade caveman.

"That was sweet!" Graham said. "It's true—we officially *rule the school*! Hey, here come two more little kids! Your turn."

When we got closer, I smiled, cleared my throat, and gave it a shot. "Hi, boys, how's it going?" I said with a cool fourth-grade smile, trying to raise one eyebrow a little higher than the other.

"Shut up, you big wiener!" yelled the smaller of the two. Then he came up to us, kicked me in the leg, and ran away laughing with his friend.

Not only did my leg hurt, but for a moment, it felt like we had suddenly shrunk back into our puny first-grade selves. That wasn't supposed to happen.

The whole time-honored-tradition thing disappeared with that one kick. It was weird . . . unnatural. We just stood there in silence.

"Wow! I wonder what went wrong." Graham scratched his head. "Maybe they were just a couple of really short third-graders or something," he said, trying to make me feel better.

I just shook my head. "I don't know, Graham. Do you think maybe I should have left it at 'Hi, boys' instead of adding the 'How's it going?' part? Maybe that was the problem," I said, rubbing my shin. "I feel cheated. It's kinda like when you've wanted something forever and your parents keep telling you, 'Maybe for Christmas.' So you wait and wait, and when Christmas finally comes, you open your presents only to find sweaters and underwear. It's not right, Graham, it's just not right." We walked back to our classroom dumbfounded, wondering what could have gone wrong.

There were name tags on all the desks. After a quick glance around the room, I found my chair. I sat next to David Miller and Brad Shaw. Heidi

Partridge sat in front of me, and Diane Dunstin was in back of me.

I was glad Diane was behind me, because if she were in front of me, I would probably never see the board. I'm one of the taller kids in my class, but Diane is the absolute tallest. She's huge, almost as tall as Mrs. Gibson, though she's not nearly as scary.

David "Big as a Gorilla" Miller was the meanest kid in the school. Sitting next to him didn't thrill me at all. But I was happy to be in back of Heidi. I kind of liked Heidi . . . you know, like a girlfriend. Only she didn't know it.

I looked around to see who else was in our class. There was Zach, the fastest kid our age. He was wearing brand-new basketball shoes, of course. Matt "The Brain" Lindenheimer was in the front row, right in front of Mrs. Gibson's desk. He's the smartest kid in the school.

I didn't dare look at Mrs. Gibson for fear she would see me. I thought I would lay low for a few days, just in case she hadn't forgotten about yesterday morning in front of the class lists yet.

The second bell rang. Mrs. Gibson's chair squeaked as she sat up straight in her chair.

"Well, let's get started, boys and girls," she said, opening her roll book and sitting down on a tall stool. "When I call your name, please respond by saying 'here'—that is, unless you are absent. In that case, please respond by saying 'not here.'"

Some of the kids who were paying attention chuckled a little. *Hey, I think she's trying to be funny,* I thought to myself. Even though I had heard that line a million times before when teachers thought they were being funny, I didn't think I would ever hear it from Mrs. Gibson.

No one laughed louder than Lizzy McQueen. Lizzy and I have been in each other's classes before. She sucks up to every teacher she's ever had. It's enough to make you sick. She says everything in a loud, whiny voice. And her face is always crinkled up, like she just smelled something stinky. Poor Graham had to sit next to Lizzy.

"That was funny, Mrs. Gibson," Lizzy said, still forcing out a fake laugh. Paying no attention to

Lizzy, Mrs. Gibson began calling out our names in alphabetical order. As she got closer to my name, I slouched down in my chair, hiding behind Heidi.

"Raymond Knudson," she called out in her scratchy old voice.

"Here," I said quietly from my hiding place. I wanted to tell her that you don't pronounce the "K" in my last name, but I thought it best to just let it go.

Mrs. Gibson paused and then called my name again.

"Here," I said a little louder, poking my head out a little.

She took off her glasses, leaned to the side, and looked me in the face. "Are you happy to be here today, Raymond?" she asked.

"*I'm* glad to be here, Mrs. Gibson!" Lizzy blurted out.

"Thank you, Lizzy, but I am speaking to Raymond," Mrs. Gibson replied, without taking her eyes off me.

"Yes, sir. I mean, ma'am— I mean, Mrs. Ma'am—

I mean, Mrs. Gibson," I said, hoping she'd move on to the next name. But no such luck. I felt sick. Heidi turned around and gave me a weird look. She probably thought I was a moron.

"I'm happy to hear that, Raymond," Mrs. Gibson continued. "I would hate to have anyone in our class who was not completely happy about being here. Sometimes students decide they don't like their teacher, even when they have never been in that teacher's class before. Raymond, do you think anyone in our class would think like that?" she asked.

"No, I don't think so," I said. My forehead was getting all sweaty.

"I don't think so, either," she said, smiling at me. "By the way, I am happy to have you in my class."

"Thank you, Mrs. Gibson. I'm glad to be here, too," I said.

"Raymond, did I pronounce your last name correctly?" she asked.

"No, ma'am, it's pronounced '*nude*-son,'" I said. "The 'K' is silent."

"'Nude' like 'naked,'" David blurted out. Everyone in the class laughed, except me. I just sweated even more.

"That's enough, David," Mrs. Gibson said. She adjusted her glasses and returned to her roll call.

David leaned over to my desk. "Why are you sweating, wimp?" he growled. "Afraid of an old lady?"

I didn't dare answer, for fear Mrs. Gibson would start talking to me again. So I just sat there quietly.

"I'm talking to you, *wimp*," David said again, only this time he included a punch to my arm.

"David, why don't you move your desk up here by mine for today? That way your long arms won't accidentally swing around and hit Raymond anymore," Mrs. Gibson said calmly. She waited for David to slide his desk to the front of the room and then continued with roll call.

Maybe Mrs. Gibson isn't so bad after all, I thought. But then again, maybe that was just what she wanted me to think. Maybe her plan was to get David mad at me so *he* would kill me. *Very sneaky,* I thought. *Getting a student to do her dirty work.* She was brilliant.

4

Revenge

I TRIED TO stay away from Mrs. Gibson as much as possible for the rest of the week. I didn't raise my hand to answer a question or ask to go to the bathroom, and I didn't volunteer for anything. As far as I was concerned, I still couldn't trust her. Every now and again, I would look up to find her squinty little eyes staring at me through those huge glasses.

When Friday came, Graham and I walked home with Diane and Heidi. I told them about what happened at the class lists the day before school started.

"So what do you guys think?" I asked them.

"What do you mean?" Diane said.

"What I mean is, do you think Mrs. Gibson is going to do something to me?" I said.

"Like what?" Heidi asked, looking confused.

"I don't know. You've heard all the stories about her," I said.

"I told him I don't think she'll do anything," Graham said. "She only looks scary because she's so old."

They all agreed and looked at me like I was crazy. "Well, maybe you guys are right," I said.

That next Monday, I decided to start raising my hand in class and to stop avoiding Mrs. Gibson. The first thing I did when we got to school was to say "Hi" to her. She gave me a crinkly smile and a raspy "Good morning." I sat down feeling a little more confident.

The bell rang and Mrs. Gibson stood up. She looked around to see who was absent, marked them in her roll book, and then walked up to the board.

"Everyone, please take out a piece of paper and

write down this week's spelling words," she said, writing ten words down the left side of the board. She gave us a few minutes to finish.

"May I have a volunteer to read the first word, tell us what it means, and use it in a sentence?" she asked.

"I'll do it, I'll do it," Lizzy yelled out, waving her hand in the air and bouncing up and down in her chair.

"Okay, Lizzy," Mrs. Gibson said.

"*Arrange. Arrange* means to put things in order," Lizzy said. "And my sentence is: Mrs. Gibson arranges the papers on her desk really good, because she is the best teacher and the best arranger."

"'Really *well*,'" Mrs. Gibson corrected. Lizzy looked surprised.

"That's what I meant, Mrs. Gibson—really *well*," she said quickly.

"Thank you, Lizzy," Mrs. Gibson said. "Can I get a volunteer for the next word?" David raised his hand. "*Strange*," he said. "*Strange* means weird, like Raymond is very strange and wears strange clothes." He sat back and laughed.

"David," Mrs. Gibson said, "why don't you pull your desk up by mine again for today."

"But I didn't hit him," David said.

Mrs. Gibson didn't answer, just waited patiently for him to move.

"Okay, next word. How about you, Raymond," she said, pointing to the next word on the board, which was *revenge*.

REVENGE? I thought. Why was she asking me to read *that* word? Maybe she was trying to tell me that she was going to get revenge on me for the things I said about her.

"Um, I don't know what it means," I said.

"I know, I know," Lizzy said, bouncing and waving again.

Mrs. Gibson waited for a few moments and then turned to Lizzy. "Okay, Lizzy, go ahead."

"Okay. *Revenge* is what you do to someone who did something mean to you, like, I am going to get revenge on that kid that was really mean to me at recess by punching him in the nose."

"Thank you, Lizzy," Mrs. Gibson said. "Let's get someone from the front of the class. How about Matt. Would you like to take the next word?"

She went on like that through all ten words without ever coming back to me. All of a sudden I felt nervous again. I didn't care what Graham, Diane, and Heidi said. Mrs. Gibson was still mad at me and was planning to do something.

Every week there seemed to be one word in the spelling list that was put in there just for me. One week it was *punishment*; other weeks' words were *bruise*, *injure*, and *damage*. Graham thought it was just a coincidence. But not me—I was so nervous that I even told my mom about it. She was making some cookies in the kitchen when I recited the whole story, starting back at the day in front of the class lists. Surely, my own mom would understand and be worried for the safety of her only son. Unfortunately, I was wrong.

"Why would you say such cruel things?" she said, putting down the big mixing spoon and turning to me. "What you need to do, young man, is go to school tomorrow and apologize for what you said."

"But, Mom," I begged, "I can't do that."

"You most certainly will. And you'll do it first thing in the morning before school," she said. "Now, up to your room."

"Okay, but if something bad happens, it's your fault," I said.

She didn't say anything, she just pointed to the stairs. I ran upstairs and threw myself onto my bed. I didn't want to fall asleep, because I knew as soon as I did, it would be morning.

Sure enough, I closed my eyes and opened them again, and it was morning. Mom already had my lunch made and was ready to drive me to school for my little chat with Mrs. Gibson. On the way, she gave me a lecture about manners and showing respect to adults. Then she gave me a kiss on the forehead and dropped me off.

I walked into the room hoping she wouldn't be there, but unfortunately she was at her desk correcting papers.

"Why, good morning, Raymond. You're here bright and early," she said.

"Yeah, I, um . . . came early to tell you that I'm sorry," I said.

"What are you sorry for?" she asked, putting her red pencil down.

Okay, here it goes, I said to myself.

And in one breath I blurted out, "You know the day before school when I was standing in front of the class lists and I, um, said a few things that maybe, um, weren't so nice about a teacher. Well, I mean, about you. I just wanted to say I'm sorry. I didn't mean what I said. It's just that I thought you were scary because everyone said you were and you looked a little scary, but I know you can't help that 'cause you're old, and so when I turned and bumped into you I was scared and have been since school started, and I don't want you to get revenge on me, so I'm sorry." I stood there trying to catch my breath.

"Have a seat, Raymond," Mrs. Gibson said. I sat down in Matt's desk.

"Raymond, I know some kids say things about me. And believe me, it's not fun getting old. But the reason I have taught school for so many years is that I enjoy working with such fine young people as you. It takes a big man to come in and apologize," she said with that wrinkly smile.

"Thanks," I said. Then I got up and turned to walk outside to wait for the other kids to arrive.

"Thank you, Raymond," she said. "I'll get you in class."

"What?" I yelled, spinning back around as a chill went down my spine.

"I said, 'I'll see you in class,'" she answered, looking confused.

"Oh, right," I said. "Yeah, see you in class." I hurried out the door and ran outside. I sat there wondering if she had really said "I'll get you in class" or if that was just my imagination. For the last six weeks I'd been waiting for her to take her revenge. But it was now the middle of October, and she hadn't done anything to me yet. I hoped it was my imagination and tried to forget about it.

Another two weeks passed by quickly, and it was November. We got our report cards for the first term. I had all As and Bs, except I got a C-plus in handwriting. Mrs. Gibson even wrote some nice comments at the bottom.

Yes, Mrs. Gibson was all right. I can't believe some kids think she's creepy. There are even kids who have never been in her class who think she's mean. Can you believe that?

Oh, well. None of that really mattered now, because we were about to participate in the biggest event at East Millcreek Elementary, the event that sets the fourth-graders apart from the rest of the unfortunate younger kids. Everything was about to change because of one word: *Scrooge!*

Each year the fourth-graders put on a play. It's always in December and it's always *Scrooge*. You know, the story about the greedy old man who is mean to everyone, and then one night he's visited by three ghosts, so he turns good and buys a turkey for Tiny Tim and his family and everyone lives happily ever after.

Scrooge is a tradition at our school. I can remember who played the part of Scrooge every year since first grade. There's also a large bulletin board in a glass case in the hall in front of the school office that has pictures from the past *Scrooge* plays. Whoever gets the part of Scrooge is famous forever at East Millcreek.

When we tried out for parts, I thought I did pretty well, and that I'd probably get the part of Scrooge. Even though I kind of forgot most of my lines, I made up some new lines that sounded even better. Mrs. Barker, who's in charge of the play, told me it was "very interesting." That must be good.

We had to list three parts we would like, just in

case we didn't get picked for the part we wanted most. Then, the next day, they were going to list the whole cast on the stage door. Graham thought he did good at his tryout, too. I hoped he'd get the part of Bob Cratchit—that way we could be in some of the same scenes together. I figured he'd probably get a good part. He and his sister were in a real play downtown last year.

When I got home, I told my mom what happened at tryouts and how Mrs. Barker thought my acting was very interesting. Mom told me acting isn't for everyone and I shouldn't get discouraged if it doesn't turn out the way I think. I wasn't worried, though. After all, if for some strange reason I didn't get the part of Scrooge, I would be happy with either of the other two parts I listed—Bob Cratchit or the ghost of Jacob Marley. Sure, they're not as important as Scrooge, but they are still good parts. I stayed awake for a long time that night, wondering which parts all my friends would get. Hopefully, no one would be mad at me for getting the part they wanted. Oh, well; I was sure they'd get over it.

5

Peter Who?

BRAD SHAW? The Brad Shaw who sits right next to me in class? The Brad Shaw with the big crazy hair and the cowboy boots? I don't get it. I just don't get it. Sure, I was a little nervous at the tryout, but I still did a good job with my new and improved lines. I couldn't believe the part of Scrooge went to Brad Shaw. And that's not all. I could live with not getting to be Scrooge. But even worse, I didn't get any of the parts I listed. Not Bob Cratchit, not even the ghost of Jacob Marley. I got the part of Peter. Yeah, you heard right: Peter. I've been watching this play since I was five years old, and I don't remember there ever being a guy named Peter in *Scrooge*.

And get this: Peter only has one line. I asked Mrs. Barker what happened. I mean, maybe it was a mistake, right? She just smiled and told me every part is important. Then she patted me on the head like you do to a dog.

Graham got the part of the younger Scrooge when he has a girlfriend. At first he didn't want the part, but when he found out Kelly D'Angelo got the part of his girlfriend, he went crazy. Graham's been in love with Kelly since the first grade. He couldn't wait to start rehearsals. He decided to ask Mrs. Barker if it would be okay if they added some kissing scenes to make the play more believable. That's pretty smart, don't you think?

After school that day, we went over to Graham's house. We usually play at his house, because most of our friends live on his street or around the corner. Heidi lives right next door to Graham. She has a swimming pool. Graham and I try to get ourselves invited to swim as often as we can in the summer. We try to be sneaky about it. Like one day last summer, we went over to her house in our swimming trunks. But to make it look like we weren't just coming over to get invited to swim, we decided to ring the doorbell and yell, "Trick or treat." We told Heidi's mom we were wearing lifeguard costumes that year. She just looked at us and said, "Trick-or-treating in July? That's creative." Then she gave us each a cookie and closed the door, with no swimming invitation. Maybe our acting was a little too good.

Diane lives in the house behind Graham's. If you look over Graham's back fence, you can see right into her yard. We go over to Diane's a lot after school, because she has a trampoline. Also, she doesn't seem like a regular girl. She's almost like the abnormally tall sister you never had. I think she looks at me and Graham like brothers, too. In fact, once we were in her room and she just started to change her clothes to go out to play, right there in front of us. She didn't even care. We couldn't believe it. We told her we'd wait outside on the trampoline. I mean, that was kinda weird.

Anyway, the day we found out what parts we got

for the school play, Graham and I walked over to Diane's house to jump on the tramp. And get this: Diane got *two* parts—the part of the narrator and one of the ghosts. I couldn't believe it. She gets two parts, while I get one measly part that no one has ever heard of. Anyway, we jumped on the tramp and talked about the play. We played follow-the-leader, where one person does a trick and we each have to try the same trick. I always lose, because they can do a backflip in layout position. That's when you do a backflip with your legs straight instead of tucking them up to your chest. I can't do a backflip like that. My knees always bend, and I get out because they say it's not the same trick they do.

After a while we sat down. Graham and Diane wanted to practice their lines for the play, so Diane went in the house to get her script. The only problem is they both had lots of lines. My *one* line only had *seven* lousy words. It went like this: "And Mother made a plum pudding, too!" Pretty bad, huh?

Diane's door slammed shut, and in no time at all she was back on the tramp with a pile of papers. She stood up in front of us and recited her lines, walking around the trampoline as if she were onstage. This went on for about ten minutes. She wasn't even close to finishing all of her lines when Graham got tired of waiting for his turn.

"Come on Diane, it's my turn," he said, grabbing the papers from her. He thumbed through the pages and finally came to his scene. We sat and listened to Graham read for a while. He actually sounded pretty good. Then my moment came. Graham passed me the script, and they both lay back on the tramp while I searched for my scene.

It was hard to find my one line in that huge pile of papers, but I finally did. I cleared my throat and began reading.

"And Mother made a plum pudding, too!" I recited.

They both looked at each other and burst out laughing.

"What?" I said. "What's so funny? So I only have one line. Big deal."

"We're not laughing at your one line," Diane said. "You're just saying it so weird. Tell us how you're really going to say it."

One line and I couldn't even do it right. They actually thought I was joking! I had to think fast.

"Yeah, I was just joking around. Pretty funny, huh?" I said, trying to laugh along, even though I had given it my best shot. "I don't know how I'm really going to say my line yet. Anyway, I have to go home." I climbed off the trampoline, put my shoes on, and headed up the street. As I walked, I recited my line over and over in my head, trying to make it sound better.

When I got home, my mom was in the kitchen making a meat loaf. I showed her my line. Surely my mom would understand my pain and humiliation. Maybe she could call Mrs. Barker and get me a different part. I would be happy being any ghost in the play at this point.

She looked at the line for a moment. Then she put on one of those pretend smiles to make me feel good and said, "What a wonderful line, Raymond!" And as she returned to smashing up the meat loaf in a big bowl, she added, "Peter Cratchit is a very important character!"

Okay, the part about the wonderful line was a lie, and I was just going to ignore it. But the part about Peter being an important character . . . get real. She couldn't be serious, could she? That was going way too far. I mean, would the play change in any way if Peter *didn't* say that Mother made a plum pudding? So what? Who cares if Mother made a plum pudding? Would the ghosts decide not to visit Scrooge if Peter's mother had not made dessert or whatever plum pudding is? Plus, why didn't they just let Tiny Tim say the "plum pudding" line? He's the only kid in that family with a good part anyway, which is another thing I was mad about. The person who got the part of Tiny Tim wasn't even a boy. It was Suzy Rivera!

I was going to get mad at my mom for telling me I had an important part, but I decided to let her off the hook this time. After all, judging from the look on her face, I think she knew how I really felt. Anyway, she's a mom, and I guess she's supposed to say things like that.

6

Who Needs Eyebrows Anyway?

THE WEEK WAS finally over. I didn't want to think about the play or anything for the weekend. I just wanted to have fun. I finished all of my homework and chores after school on Friday, so I could play all day Saturday. I woke up early Saturday and went to Graham's house, where we began our day-long fun fest.

We played Harlem Globetrotters, whistling the theme music and making crazy passes and shots. After that, we played pool, climbed the huge tree in the backyard, bugged Graham's little sister, and did every other fun thing we could think of. The only problem was that we were done by noon. While we were sitting in Graham's room thinking of what to do next, I saw a big magnifying glass lying halfway under his bed.

"Cool! Where did you get this?" I asked. I picked it up and started examining things.

"I don't know," Graham said. "I've had it forever."

I held the magnifying glass up to Graham's wall. "Hey, Graham, this looks like a booger," I said, examining the greenish-brown crumb stuck on his wall.

"That's not a booger!" Graham said. "I think it's some cereal or something."

"Yeah, right. Let's just see if we can find a match, shall we," I said. "Lean your head back and let's take a look-see." I looked through the magnifying glass into Graham's nose. "Whoa, this is disgusting!" I said. "Wait a minute. What's this? Oh my gosh, I can't believe it!"

"Okay, okay, I'll go blow my nose," Graham said, pushing the magnifying glass away. "Give me a break. I bet you have your fair share of boogers in your nose, too, Raymond."

"I'm not talking about the boogers, Graham. I think you have a mustache starting to grow. The tiny hairs are almost invisible, but you can see them in the magnifying glass."

"No way! Are you serious?" Graham said. He couldn't help smiling. He rubbed his hand over his microscopic mustache. "This is sooo cool! I guess we really are fourth-grade men. I wish it would grow in faster."

"Graham, I know what we have to do," I said, remembering what my cousin Norman once told me. "We have to shave! That's what makes your whiskers grow faster."

"Are you sure?" Graham asked.

"No, but it seems right. I mean, how could any real whiskers grow in until you get those tiny, see-through ones out of the way? Don't you think?" It made sense to me.

"Yeah, you're probably right," Graham said. "I'll go get a razor."

Graham was back in a flash. He had an electric razor in one hand and was rubbing his face with the other hand. "You know, I think I can feel it," he said. "I wonder if Kelly would like me with a mustache?"

"Probably," I said, grabbing the cord and plugging it into the wall. "You know, we should be taking a picture of this moment. I mean, it's your first shave. It's kind of like saying your first words, taking your first steps, or playing your first video game. This is huge!"

"Yeah, you're right," Graham said. "But I don't have a camera. Plus, now that I think about it, my mustache has been itching me lately, so I think I should just get it off as quick as I can." He turned the razor on and started rubbing it all over his face.

"Is it working?" I asked. "I wonder if you're doing it right."

"I'm not sure," Graham said.

"I know," I said. "Try it on a piece of your hair or something. Or better yet, try it on the very corner of your eyebrow. Eyebrows are kind of like whiskers."

"Good idea," Graham said. And without looking into a mirror, he pressed the razor onto his eyebrow.

"Hold on, Graham! Not over all of it!" I said,

pulling the razor away from his face. "Oh my gosh! It's . . . it's gone!" I said.

"What's gone?" Graham said, feeling his face.

"Your eyebrow! It's gone!"

"*What?*" Graham yelled, rubbing the bald spot that used to be his eyebrow. "Oh, no—it *is* gone! I need a mirror. I bet I look like a freak!" Graham got up and started toward the door. I followed.

"What do you think?" I asked.

"I *do* look like a freak!" Graham said in a half-mad, half-crying voice. "I can't believe this."

I didn't know what to say. The truth was he did look like a freak. But I wasn't going to tell him that.

"Wait a minute. I have an idea," I said. "My grandma doesn't have any eyebrows at all. I don't know if she shaves them off like you do or what."

"I don't shave mine off! This was the first time. It was an accident!" Graham yelled.

"I know, I know," I said. "Anyway, what I was going to say is that my grandma has some special pencil she draws eyebrows on with."

"What do you mean, 'draws eyebrows on with'?" Graham said.

"Well, she shaves hers off and then draws new ones on, I guess. I don't know why she does it," I said.

"So are you saying we should draw a new eyebrow on my face?" Graham asked.

"Yeah. Why not? I'm a better artist than my grandma. I'll bet we can give you a great eyebrow," I said. We went back into his room and looked for some colored pencils.

"How about these," I said, picking up a box of markers. I opened the box and found an orange one that seemed to match his other eyebrow pretty well.

"Be careful," Graham said.

"I will. Now, what kind should we draw? We could do an angry one that kind of points down in the middle, or a happy one that sits kind of high on your forehead," I said.

"How about you just try to draw one that looks like the other one," Graham said. "I don't want to walk around looking half angry all day long."

"Right," I said. I started drawing an eyebrow as

similar to his other one as I could. Unfortunately I drew it a little too long. It came almost to the middle of his forehead. Now his other eyebrow looked too short.

"Hold on," I said. "I'm just going to fix your real eyebrow a little to match the new one."

"What?" Graham said. His eyes were still closed.

"Don't worry. We can always wash it off if it looks bad," I said. That seemed to calm him down. The only problem was that each time I added more to one side, it looked like I needed to add more to the other side. After a few times going back and forth, I stood back to look at my work.

"Whoa," I said. "Maybe I should have had my grandma do this for you."

"What? Let me see," Graham said. He stood up and we both walked down to the bathroom. Graham looked into the mirror. His eyebrows were about four inches tall and were connected in the middle.

"Pretty good, huh?" I said.

"It's just one big, fat, long eyebrow," Graham said. I thought he was going to cry, but then out of nowhere he burst out laughing. Then I started. We stood there for about ten minutes looking in the mirror and laughing. We couldn't stop.

Finally, Graham caught his breath. "I think I'll just go with the one real one," he said. We both laughed some more as Graham washed off the gargantuan orange eyebrow.

7

Welcome, Luke

ON MONDAY MORNING, I walked down
to Graham's house to pick him up for school. He
opened the door.

"Wow," I said. "It didn't grow back yet, did it?"

Graham just gave me a stupid look. "I begged my
mom to let me stay home from school until it grows
back. But she said it's going to take a long time."

"Sorry, man," I said. "Maybe no one will notice."

"Right," Graham said.

Unfortunately, when we got to school, Graham's
missing eyebrow was all anyone could talk about.
Usually when you get a bad haircut, people will tease
you for about an hour, then they forget about it. But

let me tell you, if you shave off your eyebrow, kids will make fun of you for days. They would probably still be laughing at Graham if it hadn't been for Luke, the new kid.

Luke's first day was that Wednesday. When Mrs. Gibson asked him to stand up and introduce himself to the class, he turned a kind of greenish yellow and said he didn't feel too good. Then he threw up all over the floor.

This was great, because now the other kids had something else to make fun of, instead of Graham's missing eyebrow. The sad thing was that the poor new kid would probably go through the rest of fourth grade—and maybe the rest of his life— known as "Luke the Puke." Poor guy.

I thought a lot about Luke that day, mostly because you could still smell throw-up. As I sat there wondering how long our room would stink, a great idea popped into my brain. It was perfect. I waited until Mrs. Gibson gave us time to study on our own, then I hurried up to her desk.

"Mrs. Gibson, I've been thinking," I said.

"Yes, Raymond, what about?" she answered, looking up from the paper she was correcting.

"Well, it must be hard for Luke, you know, being new and everything," I said. "The rest of us in the class are involved in the play . . . and, well, I would hate for Luke to feel left out. I mean, he hardly knows anyone yet. So I was thinking maybe we should give him a part in the play. And since there are no more parts, I would be happy to give him mine. You know, to make him feel welcome."

"That's a great idea, Raymond, and very thoughtful," Mrs. Gibson replied.

Yes! I thought to myself. I did it. No more play. No more plum pudding. No more humiliation. I was really beginning to like that new kid. But it was too good to be true. At that moment, Mrs. Gibson called Diane up to her desk.

"Diane," she said. "Raymond has an idea to make our new student, Luke, feel welcome in our class. He thinks we should give him a part in the play. Don't you think that would be nice?" she continued, smiling at both Diane and me. "And since you have two parts, Diane, I was wondering how you would feel about giving one of them to Luke."

What? What is going on here? I screamed inside my head. I couldn't believe this was happening. She had it all wrong! Didn't she hear the part about me giving up *my* part to Luke? I mean, Luke was supposed to be the new plum-pudding guy, not the new narrator or ghost. Plus, this wasn't fair. He didn't even have to try out.

"That would be fine, I guess," Diane said, giving me a "you'll pay for this" kind of glare.

"Wonderful," Mrs. Gibson said. "I'll talk to Mrs. Barker about it after school."

This was just great. Not only did I still have my part, but I made Diane lose one of hers. I bet my trampoline-jumping days were over, too. I didn't know what plum pudding was, but I sure hated it! I went back to my desk and didn't say a word for the rest of the day.

The final school bell rang, and we all raced toward the door. Graham made it out first and was waiting for me on the front steps. As we walked home, we told each other about our problems. He told me about how he invited Kelly D'Angelo to his house to go over their lines together and she said, "No way." He thought it was because his missing eyebrow freaked her out. We discussed life's mysteries, like how long it takes for eyebrows to grow back and stuff like that.

I told him about the mess I made with Diane's parts in the play.

"So that's why she's so mad," he said. "I bet we'll never jump on the trampoline again," he added.

"Yeah. Hey, how much money do you have?" I asked.

"A dollar fifty," he said, pulling a handful of coins out of his pocket.

"I've got seventy-five cents," I said with a smile.

"Are you thinking what I'm thinking?" he asked.

"Let's go, *hermano*," I said. *Hermano* means "brother" in Spanish. We know a few words in Spanish that we only use on special occasions or when we need to get ourselves in a good mood, like now. Other words we know are *casa*, which means "house," *baño,* which means "bathroom," *dinero,* which means "money," and *bonita,* which means "pretty."

Whenever we have a bad day at school and we happen to have some extra money, which isn't very often, we walk over to The Store and buy a box of Pop-Tarts or some cookies or something. The name of the store is actually "The Store." Can you believe that? Whoever built that place couldn't think of anything better to name it than "The Store." If I built a store I would call it "Raymondo's Food Extravaganza." And I would never, ever, sell plum pudding.

I don't know what it is about Pop-Tarts, but we love them. It's not that they taste especially good. They're kind of like little cardboard squares with hard frosting on them. But they're more like a tradition with me and Graham. I think when we're old men and our wives are sitting around knitting socks or sweaters or something, Graham and I will be hobbling over to The Store to share a box of Pop-Tarts.

Anyway, that day when we got to The Store, we began walking up and down the aisles like we always do. Only this time we saw something that was both crazy and disgusting at the same time.

There on the bread shelf right next to the hamburger buns was a set of false teeth. I'm not talking about fake, Halloween-type teeth, either. These were real choppers right out of some old person's mouth. We both fell to the floor laughing.

"I'll give you my seventy-five cents if you touch them," I said.

"No way," Graham replied. "But I'll give you my whole dollar fifty if you try them on."

"Are you insane?" I said, trying to catch my breath from laughing. "Do you know what kind of disease you could get from an old person? They're always coughing, wheezing, and complaining about the way they feel. There's no way those chompers are getting close to my mouth."

We walked all over the store trying to find the old person who lost their teeth. We thought the only thing funnier than some teeth on a shelf would be someone walking around without any teeth at all. After a couple of minutes, we gave up our search,

bought our Pop-Tarts, and headed home. Usually we eat all the Pop-Tarts before we ever make it home, so we almost never get the chance to put them in the toaster like you're supposed to. But that day was different. We laughed most of the way home talking about teeth and eyebrows. Just when we finally stopped laughing and made it to Graham's street, Graham burst out laughing again.

"What is so funny?" I said. Graham could hardly control himself, he was laughing so hard.

"Wouldn't it be—?" he started, trying to catch his breath.

"Spit it out, man. What?" I wanted to know.

"Wouldn't if be funny if tomorrow at school—?" Again Graham started to crack up.

Suddenly I knew exactly what Graham was thinking. "If we saw Mrs. Gibson without her teeth?" I said, bursting out laughing.

Graham nodded his head and held his sides from laughing so hard. We laughed until our cheeks and sides hurt. We got to his house and were able to enjoy the last two tarts straight from the toaster.

8

Plum Pudding, Anyone?

THE NEXT DAY, everything seemed to go my way. Diane didn't say anything about losing one of her parts in the play, I got a Twinkie in my lunch bag, and best of all, I got an A-minus on my math test. Yes, life was good. Then came Friday.

I could tell it wasn't going to be a good day from the moment I woke up. Mom was too late to make me breakfast like she normally does. So I opened the cupboard to get some cereal, and the only kind we had was that shredded-wheat stuff that looks and tastes like little bales of hay. And it wasn't even the kind that is frosted on one side. I don't know why every kid on the planet gets to eat sugar cereals but me.

Anyway, I got to school and did badly on my spelling test, mostly because I hadn't studied. Then at lunch, I opened my lunch sack to find a sandwich made from the end pieces of the bread and a small bag with half a carrot. It only got worse from there. Our first play practice was after school. I sat in the audience most of the time thinking that we would never make it to my part. Then, after a bunch of scenes with Ebenezer Scrooge in them, it was suddenly my turn.

"Okay, let's have all of Bob Cratchit's family onstage, and we'll take it from the top of page twenty-seven," Mrs. Barker called. All of us Cratchit kids got onstage. We had to pretend we had cups of something to drink. I was pretty good at that part. Then after a couple of Tiny Tim's lines, it was my turn.

I looked out into the audience. David was sitting there making faces at me. Everyone else just stared and waited for my line. Then all of a sudden that one measly little line slipped my mind. I looked over at Mrs. Barker for some help. She was mouthing something to me, but what? She was moving her mouth big and slow. It looked like she was saying, "Meow, meow, moo, wooo," but that couldn't be right.

"*Cut!*" I yelled. "Can we do this over?"

"Sure, Raymond," she said, smiling back at me.

"By the way, could you tell me my line again?" I asked, feeling like an idiot. I mean, what kind of moron can't remember one line? After all, it had been haunting me ever since I first read it.

"'And Mother made a plum pudding, too,'" Mrs. Barker said.

"Right, right. Thanks," I said. Of course, that stupid plum pudding. How could I forget? I was ready now.

"Okay, Raymond, let's start where we left off," Mrs. Barker said, getting back up on her stool in front of the stage.

"And Mother made a plum pudding, too," I said.

There was a short pause, and then laughter came at me from all directions. Even Mrs. Barker was laughing. It seemed that *she* would at least keep her laughing to herself; after all, she was the adult there. And what was it with this stupid line? The words aren't funny. Was I that bad of an actor that these seven words sounded so ridiculous?

"Let's try that again," Mrs. Barker said, still smiling. "But this time try to be excited. This is a family that doesn't have a lot of money. Plum pudding is a treat they may only get once a year. Peter is excited to exclaim to his brothers and sisters, 'Wow! We get plum pudding!'" Mrs. Barker said, waving her arms around and opening her eyes as wide as they could open. "Try it again with that kind of energy, Raymond."

I hate this, I hate this, I hate this, I repeated in my mind. Then I took a deep breath, closed my eyes, and thought to myself, *I can do this.* And trying to get all excited inside, I said my line with as much energy as I could muster.

"And Mother made a plum pudding, too," I repeated. Even though I was trying to be excited inside, on the outside the words came out exactly the same as before. And again, the same response: laughter.

Once everybody calmed down, I called over to Mrs. Barker, "Can't I just change the words from 'plum pudding' to 'Pop-Tarts' or something that I have actually eaten before? I mean, who has ever had a plum pudding? Maybe that's my problem."

"No, Raymond, we can't change the lines of the play. Let's move on, but Raymond, I have some homework for you. I want you to spend this weekend being Peter. I want you to think about plum pudding. Perhaps you can ask your mother to make a plum pudding. You may find that it's really good. Maybe it will help you get excited. Act like Peter at home with other things. If your mother makes pancakes, run and tell your brothers and sisters, 'And Mother made some pancakes, too!'"

Maybe she was right. Maybe I couldn't act like Peter because I just didn't feel like Peter. "I'll do it, Mrs. Barker," I called back to her. She smiled, looked at her watch, and moved on to the next scene.

After practice, I walked home with Graham as usual. We practiced my line together. We used it on everything we saw. We just substituted some of the words. Like when we saw Brad Shaw trip down the school stairs, I pointed at him, put an excited look on my face, and said, "And Brad fell down the stairs, too!" It still came out like my "plum pudding" line, but the weekend was just beginning. By Monday morning I would have this Peter guy down perfect.

Diane and Heidi were walking about ten feet ahead of us. I yelled out in my Peter voice, "And Diane let us jump on the trampoline, too!"

"Not in this lifetime Peter, Peter, Part Stealer," she called back. I guess she wasn't completely over losing her other part to Luke.

"And Peter stepped in dog poop, too!" Graham interrupted in his Peter voice, which sounded much better than my Peter voice.

"What?" I said, looking down at my shoe. He was right. I had stepped right in it. When I become a famous inventor, the first thing I am going to invent is a dog toilet. I mean, it doesn't seem right that dogs just go to the bathroom wherever they want. What would happen if people did that? I bet even dogs would get upset. We spent the rest of the walk home discussing how dog toilets would change the world.

When we got to Graham's house, I spent the first twenty minutes trying to scrape the dog poop from in between the tracks of my shoes. Last time I stepped in dog poop, I just slid my feet across the grass thinking that would do the trick. But I guess it didn't come off between the tracks, because once I got home it decided to come off on the carpet instead. Mom made me scrub the carpet until all the stink was out.

After cleaning my shoe, there wasn't very much time to play, so I just walked home. I was excited to get started practicing my line on my mom. This weekend I would become Peter for sure!

While Mom put dinner on the table, I asked her if she would make a plum pudding for dessert.

"Did you say plum pudding?" she asked with a confused look on her face.

"Yes, plum pudding! It's my favorite!" I said in my very best Peter voice.

"I'm sorry, sweetie, we're having tacos and rice

tonight. But I do have ice cream for dessert," she said.

"How about plum ice cream?" I said. This wasn't going so well. "Don't we have any kind of plum food in the house?" I asked in my almost-crying voice. It's the voice I use when I want something really badly. Mom can't bear to hear me cry.

"I really am sorry, Raymond. I don't know where your sudden love of plums came from, but the only things I have that could be considered plums are the prunes in the refrigerator. I keep them for Grandpa when he visits," she said, pulling the jar of prunes out of the refrigerator. They looked like huge raisins.

"Great!" I said. "I'll take them!" I grabbed the jar and set it on the table next to my plate. Then I went upstairs to wash my hands. My twelve-year-old sister, Geri, was in her room. This would be a great time to practice.

"Hey, Ger, were having tacos and rice for dinner!" I called to her.

"Whoop-tee-doo," she yelled back. "Shut my door!"

"Okay, but guess what? Mother made a plum prune, too!" I called back, trying out my line with some real plums.

"I said shut my door, you weirdo!" she yelled back. She walked over and shut the door herself.

Yes! I said to myself. It was perfect. Sure, she yelled at me. But the best part was what she didn't do: she didn't laugh!

I ran back downstairs and poked my head into the living room. "Hey, Dad, come eat. And by the way, Mother made a plum prune, too!" I said. He lowered his newspaper and looked at me without saying anything. Again, no laughter. I was getting good at this.

Within two minutes everyone was at the table.

"What's this about prunes, dear?" he asked Mom.

"Oh, Raymond would really like to try prunes for dessert today," she said, winking at Dad. "You can have some, too, if you'd like."

Dad chuckled to himself. "As tempting as that sounds, I think I'll pass."

The tacos were great. And as soon as we finished, Mom brought out some ice cream for desert. She dished it out and passed a bowl to everyone. I ate mine as fast as I could, so I could get to the jar of prunes.

I scooped out one prune. It sure didn't look too good up close. But if this Peter guy was so excited about plums, they must be good. I sat and stared at it for a long time.

Pretty soon everyone had finished their ice cream. Geri excused herself and disappeared back upstairs. After putting his dish in the sink, Dad returned to his paper in the living room. I was still staring at the wrinkly prune on my spoon. Fortunately, the phone rang and gave me an excuse get up. It was Grandma calling for mom.

"I'll take it in the living room," she said. In a few moments I heard my mom's voice on the other side, and I hung up the phone.

It's now or never, I thought to myself. Sitting back down in my chair, I grabbed my spoon, scooped up the prune, and took a big bite. It was terrible! I was

really beginning to wonder what kind of kid this Peter was. But maybe if I just kept eating them, I would get used to them and start liking them. If it would help me say my line better, it would be worth it. I dumped the rest of the prunes into my bowl and dug in.

I ate every last one of those prunes and still hated them. I decided to give my line-practicing a break and went to the family room to play some video games.

Space Racers was my favorite video game of all time. None of my friends had even come close to beating my high score. I don't know if it was something in the prunes or what, but after about an hour of playing, I beat my all-time best score!

"*Yeah!*" I yelled, jumping up and down. "*High score!*"

"Raymond, you've been playing that game long enough. Let's turn it off," Mom called from the living room.

"Just one more game," I said. "Then I promise I'll turn it off." She didn't answer, so I figured that meant I could keep playing. As I was about to be-gin my next game, I felt something strange in my stomach. It was one of those feelings that makes you think it may be a good idea to get to a bath-room, and fast!

I paused for a moment to see if the feeling would go away. But then, out of nowhere, my hands threw down the controller and my legs started running to the bathroom all by themselves. I had no control over what my body was doing. It's like my legs knew something that I didn't, and they weren't going to wait for me to decide to run. I grabbed the door-knob, but it was locked.

"Sorry. I'll be here for a while, bud," my dad said from inside the bathroom.

I turned and ran toward the next closest bath-room. It was upstairs. I tripped over Maggie, our dog, on the way. She yelped and scurried away.

"Hey, what's going on over there?" Mom called from the living room.

"I don't know!" I screamed back, slamming the bathroom door behind me.

Fortunately my legs *had* known something I hadn't, because had I waited one more second to decide to run into the bathroom, it would have been too late.

Now I don't want to gross you out with too many details, but let's just say that I have never, ever, in the history of my life, had diarrhea like this before. It just kept coming and coming and coming. And just when I thought I was done, round two started.

Finally, after about twenty minutes, I opened the door. I took five steps toward my room across the hall, when my legs decided to take me right back to the bathroom.

After another ten minutes of grueling punishment, I again attempted to leave the bathroom. This time I made it all the way to my bedroom. I plopped myself on the bed, totally exhausted, and lay there motionless. There was a lot of gurgling and bubbling going on in my stomach. I was hoping it was my stomach's way of trying to get better.

Mom came in to check on me.

"Are you okay, dear?" she asked, putting her hand on my forehead.

"I don't know," I said. "I feel like I just exploded."

"Did you eat too much for dinner?" she asked, trying to figure out what had happened.

"No, just two tacos . . . my usual amount. I also had one glass of milk, half of my rice, and then a few prunes for dessert," I said, rolling over on my side.

"Oh, dear," she said in sort of a worried voice. "How many prunes did you have? You know Grandpa has just a couple of prunes now and then to keep him regular."

"What do you mean 'regular'?" I asked. "Grandpa always looks regular to me."

"Well, when I say 'regular,' I mean the prunes help him go to the bathroom more regularly. You know, more often," she explained as she sat down on the corner of my bed.

"What? Go to the bathroom more often?" I moaned. "Is he nuts? Why would anyone want to go to the bathroom more often? I just spent half an hour in there, and I would be happy if I didn't have to go for another month!"

"Calm down, Raymond. How many prunes did you eat?" she said in the same worried voice.

I could tell from the look on her face that eating the entire jar was probably not a good idea.

"Well, I, uh, ate all the rest of the prunes!" I said.

"You ate *all* of the prunes?" she asked with a very serious, worried look on her face.

Suddenly fear came over me. "What's going to happen?" I blurted out. "Am I going to die? Am I going to be *regular* forever? Am I going to spend the rest of my life sitting on a *toilet*? Tell me! Tell me!" I yelled, a little out of control. Okay, I was a lot out of control. But before Mom could get me calmed down, my legs were once again running me down the hall to the bathroom.

"Don't worry, sweetie," Mom told me through the bathroom door. "You should be fine by morning."

Morning? I didn't think I could make it until morning. I spent the rest of the night sleeping outside the bathroom door. It was a very long night. Mom brought me a pillow and an extra roll of toilet paper. I didn't use the pillow very much, but I sure used the toilet paper.

I made it through the night, although I didn't feel completely like myself until Monday morning.

On the way to school, I told Graham the whole story. He laughed so hard he started to cry. I didn't laugh at all.

"I thought you didn't want to come over and play Saturday because you had something better going on," he said. "When your mom told me you couldn't come to the phone, I figured you were busy doing something fun."

"Well, I was busy, that's for sure. But I definitely wasn't doing anything fun," I said. "It was something I never want to experience again as long as I live. My grandpa must be nuts to always want to be so 'regular.' Anyway, I never want to hear the word *prune* again! And that goes for *plum*, too!"

"So I guess trying to act like Peter didn't help," Graham joked.

"Nope," I answered. "But I'll bet I know why he only has one line in the play."

"Why is that?" Graham asked.

"Because he probably ate the whole plum pudding and spent the rest of the play in the bathroom being regular," I said.

We joked about being "regular" all the way to school, arriving right as the bell rang. Mrs. Gibson was standing in the doorway greeting the kids.

"Good morning, Graham. Good morning, Raymond. How were your weekends?" she asked, with that wrinkly smile.

"My weekend was great," Graham answered happily. "But Raymond's weekend was just regular," he added. We both laughed and hurried to our seats.

9

A Sick Plan

TWO MORE WEEKS passed by, and there were only two days until our performance. On the way home from school, I kept going over my line in my head. No matter how many times I said it, it still came out the same. I walked home alone because Graham had to leave school early to go to the dentist.

When I got home, I heard my mom in the kitchen talking to someone on the phone. It was my grandma. I walked in, opened the fridge, and looked for something to eat. As I stood there, I overheard my mom invite my grandma to the play. I slammed the fridge door and ran over to my mom.

"Don't do that, Mom!" I yelled, grabbing the phone. "They can't come see me! They'll drive all the way to my school to see my play, probably thinking I'm Scrooge, Cratchit, or someone important, only to learn that their grandson is stupid Peter! They shouldn't have to go through that. I mean, they're old! They should be able to spend their last few years thinking their grandson is great."

"Raymond, don't talk like that!" she said, grabbing the phone and covering the part you talk into. "She can hear you. You probably hurt her feelings, talking about how old they are. Your grandparents are still young and have more than a few years left, and they love you very much. They will be just as proud as I will to see you as Peter in your school play. Now run along and we'll talk about this later."

"Fine!" I said. "Go ahead and invite them. If they get so upset that they have to be put in the old-people's home after the play, don't blame me." Mom gave me the "You're in trouble" look. Then she got back on the phone and apologized for my rudeness.

Rudeness? I thought to myself. What was she talking about? I was only trying to spare them the heartbreak of seeing their grandson make an idiot of himself in front of the whole world. I didn't know what else I could do, but somehow I had to find a way out of this play. Maybe something would come to me in a dream.

The next morning I woke up more nervous than

ever. I still had no plan on how to get out of this play, and now it was the day before the performance. I ate some oatmeal and headed down to Graham's to pick him up for school.

"Can you believe it's almost here?" Graham said. "I can't wait. For a brief couple of minutes, Kelly has to pretend she's my girlfriend, and in front of tons of people, too!" I could tell Graham was in another world.

"I just want it to be over with," I said. "I mean, you get to have the girl you love love you back, while I, on the other hand, get to stand up in front of all those people, including my grandparents, and exclaim to the world how much I love plum pudding. It's just not fair." I stopped walking for a moment to let the whole unfairness of it all sink in.

"There's still time to get out of this! Let's think, Graham. There must be something simple we're overlooking."

"How about you eat another bunch of prunes the day of the play?" Graham said. "Then when the play is about to begin, you won't be able to leave the bathroom."

"Do you know what kind of reputation I'll get if I miss the school play because I have diarrhea? That would be more humiliating than the 'plum pudding' line," I said.

"Too bad you can't just fake sick," Graham said. "But that would be too obvious. Your mom would never buy it."

"Graham, you're a genius!" I said. "It would only be too obvious if I really were faking. What if I actually get sick for real today? This is perfect. When we get to school, help me spot every person who has a runny nose, a cough, a sneeze, an itch, or anything else sickly or disgusting."

Graham looked at me like I was nuts. "Whatever you say, *hermano*."

We got to school about ten minutes early. I hung up my coat and walked outside to wait for the first bell.

"Where's your coat, son?" Mr. Scott, a third-grade teacher, said. "You're going to catch a cold."

I just smiled and pretended to walk back into the building. But when Mr. Scott turned the corner, I went back outside. I stayed out until the first bell rang. After I got to my desk, I took a careful look around the class to see if anyone looked sick.

Aha! I said to myself: Lizzy McQueen. Lizzy had a handful of tissues, and she was all red and sore under her nose, a sure sign of a cold. Plus, she had been out sick the day before. I had to get close to her, but how? Lizzy and I weren't exactly friends. In fact, she drove me nuts. Her whole teacher's-pet thing was just obnoxious. And that fake laughing at anything that resembled a joke from Mrs. Gibson was enough to make me puke. But I had to look beyond all of that. I was on a mission to get sick, and Lizzy was carrying the germs I needed to complete that mission.

I made my plan. Step one: anything that Lizzy touched, I would touch. Step two: I had to drink out of her straw at lunch. Step three: while I never thought my first kiss would be with Lizzy, I would have to find a way to kiss her. If for some reason the first two didn't work, surely a kiss would do the trick.

The rest of the morning, I kept my eye on Lizzy

and everything she touched—her books, her desk, her pencil. She was actually chewing on her pencil. It was perfect. When morning recess finally came, I waited for everyone to leave the classroom. Once they were gone, I walked by Lizzy's desk. Quickly and quietly, I reached into her desk and grabbed the gnawed pencil. I stuck it in my mouth and chewed on it myself. *Step one complete,* I said to myself, and I went out to play—with no coat on, of course.

After recess, time seemed to stand still. Step two could only be completed at lunch. I spent all of math and spelling thinking about what I would do. There were two problems. One, I had to sit near Lizzy, which meant I would have to find a way to sit at the table Lizzy and all of her Lizzy-type friends sit at, which was not the table I, or any of my friends, ever sat at. And two, I would need to drink out of her straw without her seeing.

I still hadn't come up with the solution for these two problems when the lunch bell rang. I grabbed Graham by the arm and explained why we had to sit by Lizzy today.

"Oh, man!" Graham said. "You're on your own with this one, buddy. There's no way I am sitting with those freaks. It's bad enough I have to sit by her in class."

"C'mon, Graham, do it for me," I begged. "Plus, I've also been figuring out a way I can kiss her. If you help me, I'll tell you what it is. Maybe it will help you get a kiss from Kelly, too." I saw Graham's eyes light up, and I knew I had him.

"All right," he said. "But as soon as you drink out of her straw, I'm gone. Okay?"

"Thanks, *hermano*! You're the best. We'll do it fast. I promise." We hurried down the hall and ran into the lunchroom. Graham buys his lunch, so he had to wait in the lunch line. Since I always bring my lunch, I walked right in. Lizzy also brought her lunch, and she went straight to her usual table and sat down. Her flock of snooty friends were in line behind Graham. I dashed over and scooched in next to Lizzy.

"Hey, what are you doing? This is *our* table," she said, giving me a nasty glare. "You never sit here. Go find your own place," she added.

"But . . ." I said, trying to think of an excuse to sit there. Finally, Graham came to my rescue.

"Excuse me, is this seat taken?" he said with a big smile. Graham was always more smooth with the girls than I was.

"Yes, these seats *are* taken. They're always taken, by me and my friends!" Lizzy said.

I was still trying to think of anything to say, when Graham continued talking.

"I'm sorry. We know that you usually sit here, but when you were absent yesterday, Mrs. Gibson asked everyone if they would do her a favor and sit with people they normally don't sit with at lunch. She said she wants everyone in the class to get to know each other better." Graham knew Lizzy would do anything Mrs. Gibson said.

Lizzy looked around quickly to make sure Mrs. Gibson didn't see her getting upset at us for wanting to sit with her and her friends. "Well," she said, "I didn't mean you couldn't sit here. I just meant that even though *we* usually sit here, today we want to share this table with you and Raymond. You know, to get to know you better." She put on that fake smile and made room for Graham and me. Then she waved at Mrs. Gibson, who was standing by the door.

Graham smiled at me. He really was a genius. I couldn't have pulled that one off without him. One by one, her snooty friends all sat down.

"What are *they* doing here?" her friend Bridgett asked out loud, as if we couldn't hear.

"It's okay, just ignore them," Lizzy said, taking a small bite out of her sandwich.

She ate her lunch slowly . . . extremely slowly. And she had to wipe her runny nose after every bite. It was disgusting. She and her friends did more talking than eating. You couldn't shut them up.

Finally I said, "Lizzy, you must be thirsty after all that talking. Would you like me to get you a straw?"

She pulled a straw from her lunch bag and waved it in front of my face. Then she continued talking, and talking, and talking with her friends. Our friends had finished eating and were already out on the playground. But not us—we were waiting for

Lizzy. All I needed was for her to open her drink, stick in the straw, and put it in her sickly, cold-infested mouth.

With five minutes left of lunch recess, she took out her drink. It was one of those miniature juice cans. Even her drink looked snooty. She shook it for about a minute before opening it. Graham's head was facedown on the table. I think he was asleep. She took one sip and put the entire can into her sack. "Let's go, girls," she said, getting up from the table.

"Wait!" I said, trying to think of a way to get those germs from her straw to my mouth. "Let me throw your sack away for you."

Lizzy gave me a strange look, set her garbage on the table, flipped her ringlet-curled hair, and left. She and her friends looked back at me and giggled as they left the lunchroom. I didn't care, though. I finally had the germs. Ripping into the bag, I pulled out her mostly full drink with her straw still in it and quickly drank the rest. I even wiped my mouth with her used napkin. Surely I would wake up the next morning with a nasty flu or some other kind of sickness. But to be certain, I needed to take the third step: The Kiss. It grossed me out just thinking of it.

The rest of the afternoon passed by quickly. During reading time, Mrs. Gibson got called down to the office. As soon as she was out the door, Graham came over to my desk. He was bugging me to tell him my plan to get Lizzy to kiss me.

"Okay, follow me," I said, walking to the back of the room. "This is how it works. Remember last spring just before our championship baseball game, when everyone was laughing at me?"

"You mean when your mom came into the dugout and kissed you?" Graham said. "Of course I remember that—you almost got laughed off the team. Even the coach was laughing. Remember when the other team's pitcher blew you a kiss your first time up to bat? That was classic."

"Yeah, yeah, yeah," I said. "But do you remember *why* she kissed me?"

Graham's face suddenly turned serious. "Listen,

Raymond," he said, "you told me this was going to be a plan to get Kelly to kiss me, not to get my mom to kiss me! Please tell me I didn't spend all of my lunch with Lizzy and her weirdo friends just to find out how to get a kiss from my mom."

"Settle down," I said, grabbing him by his shoulders. "Just answer the question. Do you remember what my mom said right before she kissed me?"

"No, I have no idea what she said. Why? What's your point?" Graham asked. He still had a serious look on his face.

"My point is my mom walked into the dugout and said, 'A kiss for luck,' and then she kissed me."

"So what? Are you saying that if your mom kisses me, I'll have good luck with Kelly? That's crazy. Remember what happened to you during that baseball game? You struck out three times, you got hit in the eye with the ball, and to top it off, you sat in that huge wad of gum," Graham said.

"Just listen!" I said. "My plan is not to have my mom kiss you! My plan is to give Lizzy a kiss for *good luck*! You know, for the play. It'll be perfect. I'll do it right after school."

"What makes you think she's going to let your lips anywhere close to hers?" Graham said. "In case you haven't noticed, Lizzy doesn't really seem to enjoy your company."

"I know, I know," I said, "she actually hates me. I've known that since the first grade, when I said her lunch stunk—which, by the way, it did. That egg-salad sandwich—or whatever it was—was foul! But who cares? Before she has time to even think about it, I'll already have her germs dancing all over my lips."

"Okay, Raymond," Graham said, "let's say that by some miracle this works. You kiss Lizzy, you get sick, and you get out of the play. There's just one thing you've forgotten. Me! What about Kelly and me? How does this get Kelly to kiss me?" Graham looked extremely frustrated.

"Don't worry, Graham," I said. "If it works for me, it will work for you."

Suddenly a light turned on in Graham's brain

and a smile stretched across his face. "You're right! A kiss for luck," he said. "How could anyone not want a little extra good luck before the biggest moment of their elementary-school career? I'm going to do it right after school."

"Me, too," I said. "Just think, Graham—I'll get the sickness I've been dying for, and you'll finally get to kiss the girl you've been in love with for the past three years. Things are really looking up, *hermano.*"

10

The Kiss

MRS. GIBSON RETURNED from the office, and we all had to get back to work. I had a hard time concentrating. All I could think about was step three: The Kiss. I mean, I'd never actually kissed a girl before, nor did I want to . . . unless it was Heidi. That might be okay. But I guess sometimes a kid has to do what a kid has to do.

After a grueling couple of hours of science and social studies, the bell finally rang. School was over. *You can do it, Raymond, you can do it!* I repeated over and over in my mind.

Just after the bell rang, Mrs. Gibson called Lizzy back to her desk. "Lizzy, here is the quiz you missed while you were out sick yesterday. Could you stay after school a few minutes to take it? I would like to get it recorded before Christmas break."

"Of course I can. It would be my pleasure," Lizzy said. She grabbed the test and strolled back to her desk.

Oh, great, I thought. *I've got to wait for her to take her stupid quiz. Now what am I going to do?* Then it hit me. *I'll spy on Graham to see how it goes with him and Kelly. By the time Graham gets his kiss, hopefully Lizzy will be done.*

Kelly was already in the hall before Graham could even get his backpack. He pushed through the other kids and made his way to the door as fast as he could. I followed close behind.

I could see Graham darting around other kids and jumping up and down, trying to see over the crowd. Just as it seemed he had missed his chance, the crowd finally thinned and the hall was clear. Kelly was standing down by the office. But unfortunately, she was with someone, and not just any someone. She was standing by her *mom.* Her mom had her hand resting on Kelly's shoulder and was talking to the principal, Mr. Worley.

I ran up to Graham. "This stinks! What's her mom doing at school?"

"I don't know," Graham said. "She's talking to Mr. Worley."

"You know, maybe it's just not meant to be," I said.

"Oh, yes it is," Graham said, not taking his eyes off of Kelly. "Wish me luck, *hermano*. I'm going in." And he walked straight up to Kelly and her mom.

I couldn't believe it. I stayed back a little, pretending to buy a pencil from the pencil machine in the hall.

"Hi, Kelly," Graham started.

"Hi, Graham," Kelly replied.

"I wanted to wish you good luck tomorrow in the play. I think our scene will be great," Graham said.

"Yeah, I hope so," Kelly replied.

Graham looked up at Kelly's mom, who was still talking to Mr. Worley. "Well, Kelly," he said, "I

would like to offer you a kiss for luck for the play."
He didn't even look scared or nervous.

Kelly stood there with a blank look on her face.
I don't think she knew what to say. Finally she
shrugged her shoulders and said, "Well . . ."

Graham didn't wait for her answer—he just immediately moved in to make good on his offer. This
was going perfectly. I couldn't believe one of my
plans was actually working! I only hoped it would
go as smoothly for me and Lizzy.

Being shorter than Kelly, Graham got on his tip-
toes. Then he tiptoed a little closer to her, closed
his eyes, and leaned forward. I think closing his
eyes was his only mistake, because just as Graham's
puckered lips were about to touch Kelly's, her mom,
who was still talking to Mr. Worley, pulled Kelly
closer to her, and instead of kissing Kelly on her
lips, Graham kissed Kelly's mom on her arm.

Fortunately, Graham's eyes were still closed. After the kiss, Graham pulled his head away, and in
one motion turned and started skipping and singing down the hall, eyes closed and all. I couldn't be-

lieve it; he thought he really kissed Kelly! I've never seen a smile as big as the smile I saw on Graham's face that day. It was like someone was pulling on both sides of his mouth as hard as they could.

I looked back at Kelly. Her mom looked down at her and then up at Graham skipping down the hall. "Did that boy kiss my arm?"

Kelly shrugged and smiled.

Mr. Worley, on the other hand, had just noticed Graham skipping and singing down the hall. "Stop, young man!" he yelled after Graham. "No running in the hall! Come back here! And stop that singing, too!" But Graham was in his own world and didn't hear a word Mr. Worley said. He just kept on skipping.

Even though he kissed Kelly's mom's arm, it still gave me the confidence I needed to kiss Lizzy's sickly, gross lips. I ran back to our classroom to see if Lizzy was done with her test.

"I forgot something in my desk," I said to Mrs. Gibson as I sat down. I dug into my desk, pretending to look for something.

I watched Lizzy finish her test and make her way back to Mrs. Gibson's desk. Even on regular days, she always stayed later than the other kids just so she could talk to Mrs. Gibson. She would either comment on what a great teacher she was, or how smart she was, or even how nicely her clothes matched that day. Lizzy is so weird. But who cared? I knew my moment was close at hand. I waited patiently at my desk while she turned in her test and did her final sucking up for the day. I was hoping she would make it quick—our final rehearsal started in fifteen minutes, and Mrs. Barker said we had to be there on time, just as if it was the real play. Fortunately, Mrs. Gibson didn't even let her get started.

Just as Lizzy approached her desk, Mrs. Gibson, without lifting her head from the papers she was grading, said, "Lizzy, I appreciate whatever kind remarks you have for me today, but I do have quite a bit of work to do, so perhaps you could save them for tomorrow."

"Of course, Mrs. Gibson. I understand completely.

I was just going to tell you that the math problems you taught us today were *soooo* interesting! I was also going to tell you that those earrings you're wearing are very fashionable, and when I'm old, I'm going to wear some just like them. But I'll wait until tomorrow to tell you all that. By the way, Mrs. Gibson, the only other thing I was going to tell you was—"

"Good-bye, Lizzy," Mrs. Gibson interrupted, still not lifting her head.

"Right. Sorry. I'll be going now. I won't take any more of your time telling you things like—"

"Lizzy, *please!*" Mrs. Gibson interrupted again. This time she put her pencil down and looked directly at her. I could tell by Lizzy's silence that she knew Mrs. Gibson was serious. She slowly turned around without saying another word and walked straight toward the door. She looked like she was about to cry.

"Lizzy!" I called, getting up from my desk and following her into the hall. She ignored me and kept going.

"Hey, wait up. I need to talk to you," I called again, without any response. I knew I needed a better strategy.

"Come on! I want to tell you something about Mrs. Gibson." By this time, Lizzy was halfway to the auditorium for our last play practice, but the second I mentioned Mrs. Gibson's name, she stopped and turned.

"What about Mrs. Gibson?" she said, putting her hands on her hips and walking toward me. She looked mad.

"Well," I started, "I . . . um . . . just wanted to say . . . that . . . I really think you are Mrs. Gibson's favorite student. Yes, that's what I wanted to say," I continued, hoping she would buy it.

Immediately, her eyebrows raised and she ran up to me, grabbed my shoulders and shook me. I could feel her fingernails digging into my shoulders.

"Why are you saying that, Raymond? What do you know?" she screamed.

I pried her fingernails out of my skin. "Relax, Lizzy, relax. I'm just saying that the way she treats you, it's clear you're her favorite student. She obviously thinks you're smart. And I just wanted to say good luck in the play tomorrow. I mean, it would be *sooo* sad if you forgot your lines and crushed that perfect image Mrs. Gibson has of you. You know, the image of being the smartest person in the class. That's all I wanted to say. Oh, except for one thing. I was wondering if I could give you . . . uh . . . maybe . . . a . . . small kiss for, um, luck. You know, just for luck. Not because I want to, but just to make sure you say your lines perfectly in front of Mrs. Gibson." I stopped and waited to be slapped, screamed at, or even laughed at.

"Raymond," Lizzy said, looking straight into my eyes, "you know I don't really like you. Not even a little. But that is the nicest thing you've ever said to me, and even though it will make me sick to my stomach to kiss you, I accept your offer. But don't get any ideas—this is strictly for Mrs. Gibson's benefit. I would hate to disappoint her."

Lizzy stopped talking, closed her eyes, and stuck out her puckered-up lips. It was so easy. She fell for it completely. I just stood there for a moment looking at those thin, sickly lips. *I can't believe I'm doing this,* I thought to myself. I moved closer to her, gave a quick glance around to make sure no one would see us, closed my eyes, and pressed my lips hard against Lizzy's so I could get as many germs as possible.

I kissed her for about two seconds just to make sure the germs had a chance to stick.

That should do it, I thought to myself. But before I had a chance to pull my lips off Lizzy's, I heard someone call my name.

"Raymond? What are you doing?" It was a familiar voice. The fear and humiliation of someone seeing me kissing Lizzy hit me like a slug in the gut from David.

Immediately, I ripped my lips away from Lizzy's and turned around only to find Heidi standing in back of us. My heart sank as my good luck suddenly turned to bad. I opened my mouth to say something, but nothing came out.

"Lizzy?" she said. "What are you guys doing?"

Lizzy and I looked at each other, and I could

tell she was feeling the same embarrassment.

"Nothing!" we both blurted out at the same time.

"Just a kiss for good luck," I finally said. I tried to smile, but it felt like I was trying to make my face do something it didn't want to do.

Heidi shook her head, turned, and walked away. I couldn't believe it. Of all the people to see me, it had to be Heidi. That stupid "kiss for luck" thing! Nothing ever seemed to work for me. Lizzy and I stood there for a moment in silence. I looked at her. She still looked embarrassed.

"Well, Lizzy," I said, watching Heidi disappear around the corner, "good luck in the play. I'm sure you'll do great. I guess we'd better get to practice." I turned and headed toward the auditorium.

I didn't say a word to Heidi or anyone at play practice. All I could think about was how weird this whole day was. Eating lunch with Lizzy, kissing Lizzy. I knew by tomorrow, everything would be the same as before with her. I mean, after all, she does bug me like no other, and I know she will always hate me just as she has since the first grade. What I was worried about, though, was Heidi. I've liked Heidi almost as long as I've hated Lizzy, and I was beginning to think maybe she liked me, too. But now, after seeing me kissing Lizzy, I'll bet she won't want to have anything to do with me.

When I got home, I ate dinner and went straight to bed, wondering just how sick I was going to be when I woke up. Hopefully, I wouldn't wake up in the middle of the night puking or anything. The best would be if I could just have a good night's sleep and get my sickness about ten minutes before I woke up.

I lay there thinking about how life doesn't seem to happen quite the way you expect. I mean, this was the year to rule the school, the year I would have my picture taken as Scrooge displayed in the hall with all the past famous fourth-graders. As I laid there deep in thought, I closed my eyes for one quick moment. When I opened them again, I was amazed to find it was morning. I was even more amazed to find that I was NOT SICK AT ALL!

11

Faking Sick

YES, I WAS feeling just fine. Not a sniffle, not a cough, not even a slight tickle in my throat. I couldn't believe it. Normally I spend all winter with those little red sores underneath my nose. You know, the kind you get from wiping your nose so many times. This year I actually kiss a sick girl, giving her germs free rein over my body, and I can't even produce a sniffle.

Oh, well—I guess I'll just have to fake it, I thought to myself. After all, it wouldn't be the first time. I usually get about two to three free sick days a year from faking. What kid doesn't? But this time it would need to be good. With Grandma and Gramps coming, I needed something more than a mere cold, more than a sniffle or a headache. I needed *a fever!*

No parent can say no to a fever. A fever is what separates the common cold from the serious, contagious, stay-home-from-school, big-daddy sicknesses. I heard David once brag about how he put the thermometer under hot water when his mom wasn't watching to fake a fever, and it worked perfectly. And if there is anyone who knows how to do something sneaky, it's David.

So I put on the sickest face I could, walked slowly down the hall, dragging my feet, and went to the kitchen. Mom was cooking oatmeal on the stove.

"Mom, is that you?" I groaned.

"Of course it's me—open your eyes, sweetie," she said.

"Sorry, I just don't feel good. I'm a little dizzy, my stomach hurts, and I think I might have a fever." I groaned a little louder.

Mom set her spoon down. "Oh, dear, not today. Your grandparents will be so disappointed. They're coming for the play tonight." Mom looked so sad, I started to feel a little guilty. But I knew I couldn't back down.

Mom felt my head. "You don't feel too warm," she said. "But better safe than sorry. I'll get the thermometer."

Mom went to her bathroom to find the thermometer. As soon as she was out of sight, I jumped up, did a little dance, and quietly sang a little song. "No play for me, no, no, no, no play for me, no siree." Then in an instant, my fiesta dance was cut short.

"What are you doing, freak?" interrupted Geri, who appeared out of nowhere.

Before I could answer, Mom was back with the thermometer.

"Mom, Raymond is dancing around the kitchen and acting like a weirdo," Geri blurted out, giving me a nasty glare.

"He may not be feeling like himself, Geri. I'm checking him for a fever," Mom said, sticking the thermometer into my mouth.

I adjusted the thermometer a little and dragged my feet down the hall to the bathroom. I closed

the door and immediately turned on the hot water. *This is going to be perfect!* I thought to myself. I stuck my finger under the running water until it got hot. Then I stuck the thermometer in the water for about a minute. It got so hot I couldn't put it back in my mouth, so I just carried it in my hand.

I stumbled back to the kitchen and handed the

burning thermometer to my mom. She held it up, twisting it back and forth to find the line. She examined it for a long time without saying a word. Any moment now I expected her to rush me to bed, give me some medicine, and perhaps even call the doctor. But she just kept staring at the thermometer.

"What does it say?" I said, breaking the silence. "Do I have a fever?"

"Well, Raymond, your temperature is a little over one hundred twelve degrees," she said. She looked like she was trying to keep from smiling.

"Wow, that seems kind of high, doesn't it?" I asked.

"Well, with a temperature that high, I don't know if you could still be alive. I've never seen a temperature that high in my life," Mom said. "There are only two things we can do. One, we take you to the hospital. They can stick you with a lot of needles, take blood from you, and maybe hook you up to some machines until they find out what could be giving you such a high fever. Or two, you could get dressed, go to school, perform your part in the play tonight, and make your parents and grandparents proud of you. So what will it be?" she asked, putting the thermometer back into the case and going back to her cooking.

Geri stuck her face about one inch from mine. "Busted, freak!" she said, laughing. "I knew you were faking."

One hundred twelve degrees, I thought to myself. How was I supposed to know that would be too high? I should have asked David what temperature he used when he pulled this off. I stood there in the kitchen wondering what to say. But the look on Mom's face told me it was probably best to go get dressed and pretend this whole faking-sick thing never happened. So that's just what I did.

When I got to Graham's house on the way to school, he was already at the curb waiting for me. He had the same smile on his face that he had after he kissed Kelly's mom's arm. I hadn't talked to Graham at all since the whole thing happened. I wondered if I should tell him who he really kissed.

But before I even had a chance to say "hi," Graham exploded with a recap of what he described as his best fourth-grade day yet.

"Raymond, can you believe it? It was just as we planned! It was the greatest! I really owe you one, *hermano*! And I was nervous—I mean, really nervous. But as soon as I closed my eyes, all my fears went away. And her lips, they were *sooooo* soft."

Looking at Graham relive the moment and seeing him so happy made it impossible to tell him the truth. "That's great," I said. "I'm really happy for you."

After replaying the moment about five more times, Graham asked how it went with me and Lizzy. I explained the whole thing to him, how I didn't get sick and how I couldn't even fake sick.

"I don't think there's anything left I can do to get out of this play," I said. "I can't get sick on purpose, I can't fake sick. I might as well just give up and face the humiliation tonight."

"I talked to Heidi at play practice," Graham said, changing the subject. "You know she saw you kissing Lizzy, don't you?"

"I know, I know," I said. "This play is ruining every part of my life. What did she say about it?" I asked.

"Not much," Graham answered. "She just said it was really weird. And she asked me if you liked Lizzy, like a girlfriend."

When Graham said the word *girlfriend*, I stopped flat in my tracks. "Well, what did you say? You didn't tell her I like Lizzy, did you?" I shouted.

"No way! Relax, man! I told her it was just a kiss for good luck," Graham said.

"Do you think she believed you? It probably looked like more than just a kiss for good luck," I said.

"Whoa, whoa, hold on a minute," Graham said. He grabbed me by the shoulders. "What do you mean it looked like more than just a kiss for good luck? What happened between you and Lizzy?"

"Nothing happened. It was just, I don't know . . . weird. I kissed her, and then I realized I didn't know how to end a kiss. You know, it just seemed to go on and on and on. And then out of nowhere,

Heidi showed up. So what else did she say?"

"Well, she didn't really say anything else. She just seemed really sad," Graham said.

My mind started racing. "Really sad, eh? Maybe that means she likes me and felt sad seeing me kissing another girl. What do you think, Graham?" I asked.

"Well, there's only one way to find out. You should just ask her," he said casually. To Graham, asking someone if they like you is as simple as asking them for the time of day.

"Yeah, right," I said. "There is *no* way I could ever do that. What if she says she doesn't like me—or worse, what if she says she *does* like me? *Then* what would I do? What am I supposed to say? 'Oh, you *do* like me? Well, that's great. Thanks for the information, I was just checking.' It just doesn't work that way for me."

"Sure it does," Graham replied. "If you can walk up to Lizzy and ask her if you can kiss her, surely you can ask Heidi if she likes you."

"Well, it's not the same with Lizzy. I didn't care

if she said yes or no. I don't care if Lizzy likes me or hates me. She's just Lizzy. Heidi is different," I said, shaking my head.

"Come on, *hermano*," Graham said. "It's the only possible way."

"I'll think about it, Graham," I said, knowing deep down I would never be able to do it.

"That's my man," Graham said, patting me on the shoulder. "It'll be easy," he continued. "I'll walk you through the whole thing." I could tell Graham was excited. After all, he was a pro at asking girls those kinds of questions, even though he had never had a girl say she liked him back.

I spent the whole school day counting down the hours until the play. I finally realized there was no way I could get out of being Peter. It was fate, or destiny, or something like that. No matter what, the play was going to happen. There was nothing left to do but accept the fact that I would soon become known throughout the history of East Millcreek as the worst actor ever.

Then it hit me. What did I have to lose? Graham

was right. I was going to look like an idiot anyway, so why not completely humiliate myself and ask Heidi if she liked me? Nothing had gone right so far anyway this year. Suddenly a happy feeling came over me, and I felt like I could do anything.

12

Lights, Camera, Action!

I WAS IN a great mood as I walked home with Graham. "You were absolutely right," I told him. "I'm going to walk straight up to Heidi and ask her if she likes me."

"Now you're talking," Graham said. "Trust me, it will work. Even if she says no, you'll still survive. Look at me—I've been asking girls if they like me for years. So far they've all said no, and I've survived."

"Tonight, backstage, right before the play, I'm going to do it," I said. I felt a new burst of energy. I still didn't know what I would do if she said yes, but somehow that didn't matter. I was sure I would figure it out.

Graham gave me a pep talk all the way to his house. That was just what I needed. Then he gave me a pat on the back and said, "Good luck, *hermano*," and went inside.

Heidi lives next door to Graham, so I gave myself my own pep talk as I passed by. Nobody was around, so to psyche myself up, I pointed at her house and yelled, *"Do you like me?"* It felt great to say it out loud. In fact, it felt so great that I thought I would say it again. *"I said, 'Do you like me?'"* It was good practice, even though no one was around. At least I thought no one was around.

Unfortunately, right after I yelled, *"Do you like me?"* for the second time, Heidi's mom stepped out from behind the bushes where she was hanging Christmas lights.

"Of course I like you, Raymond," she said with a smile.

I almost jumped out of my shoes. "Um, I was, I mean, I didn't, I mean, I gotta go," I said in a quivery voice.

Heidi's mom was still smiling. I was not. Why did I have to say it so loud, "projecting" like Mrs.

Barker instructed us to do when we're onstage? First, Heidi sees me kissing Lizzy. Next, I ask her mom if she likes me.

I ran home and went straight to my room. As bad as things were going, I was still determined to talk to Heidi at the play. Over and over in my head, I recited what I would say to her. It would go something like this: "Hello, Heidi. May I have a moment of your time? You see, I am very concerned that you saw me kissing Lizzy, and perhaps you are thinking that I like her, when I was actually only kissing her for good luck. There is only one person I really like, and that person is you. I was wondering if you like me, too?" Yes, that's what I was going to say. After rehearsing it a million more times, it was time for dinner. As I walked to the kitchen, the doorbell rang.

"I'll get it," I yelled. It was Grandma and Grandpa coming over for dinner before the play. They both had big smiles on their faces.

"Why, hello there. If it isn't Mr. Alastair Sim," Gramps said, shaking my hand.

"Who's that?" I asked.

"Only the most famous actor to ever play the part of Ebenezer Scrooge, my good fellow," he said happily.

"Really?" I said. "Do you remember who played Peter?"

"Peter who?" Gramps asked. He obviously had never heard of the part of Peter.

"Never mind," I said. We all walked into the kitchen and sat down.

I was so nervous I couldn't eat much. After I played with my food for a while, Mom told me I had better get ready to go. I got dressed in my Peter clothes, and Mom took my picture in the living room. Then we drove down to the school in two cars. I went with Grandma and Gramps. I probably could have walked faster than Gramps drove, but that's okay. We finally arrived, and I jumped out and ran in the front door. I wanted to talk to Heidi while I was still feeling brave.

I ran down the hall, dodging kids and parents. As I turned the corner, I saw her. And luckily for me, she was all alone. This was perfect.

"Heidi!" I said, running up to her.

She turned toward me and waved. "Hi, Raymond." Heidi was Bob Cratchit's wife. She looked cute in her costume.

Suddenly I forgot the lines I had been practicing all afternoon. It felt like the first day of play practice all over again. I decided to do the best I could.

"Heidi . . . hi . . . I . . . uh . . . just wanted you to know that . . . well . . . I was kissing . . . um . . ." This was not going as smoothly as Graham promised. "Okay, let me start over," I said, looking into her confused eyes. "You . . . you probably don't care that I was kissing Lizzy. I mean, I don't know if you care, but if you did care . . . I mean . . . well . . . it doesn't matter. I just wanted to tell you that I don't like her. I was just giving her a good-luck kiss for the play. You know, a good-luck kiss. You've heard of that, right? It was just a kiss for good luck. You know, for the play." I stopped talking to catch my breath. Heidi's confused look slowly changed to a smile.

"Well," Heidi said, "I didn't know you were giving out good-luck kisses for the play. I could use a little good luck," she continued. She smiled even bigger and took one step toward me.

Suddenly my mind went blank, and I started to feel dizzy. None of this was in the plan. I looked at Heidi, who had taken one more step toward me. *My luck is finally changing,* I thought to myself. *Maybe kissing Lizzy turned out to be a real good-luck kiss for me.*

But as I leaned in to kiss her, I heard a loud clap next to my ear. It was Mrs. Barker.

"Places, everyone! Places!" she said, still clapping.

Heidi jumped back and the moment was gone. She hurried to get to her place backstage.

But as she was going, she turned to me and said, "How about after the play?"

"Okay!" I said loudly. Then I thought to myself that she really wouldn't need any good luck for the play once the play was over. Then I thought, *You moron, who cares, are you going to pass up a kiss from Heidi on a technicality? Of course not.*

Mr. Worley walked out and welcomed the

audience. Then the lights went dim and the play began. It seemed to be going great. The audience clapped after each scene and laughed at all the parts they were supposed to laugh at. From my spot on the side of the stage, I could see proud parents' faces smiling as they watched another year's tradition go down in history.

Graham was walking around backstage rehearsing his lines. He sounded like a real professional actor. I knew he would do a great job. Mrs. Barker told him his scene was next. Graham answered in his young Ebenezer Scrooge voice and confidently walked up to the edge of the curtain to wait for his scene.

Just then Kelly came up and tapped him on the arm.

"Yes, Belle," he said to her, still in his Ebenezer voice. Belle was Kelly's name in the play.

"Graham," Kelly said. "I need to ask you something."

"Anything, my dear Belle. And please call me Ebenezer," Graham replied.

Wow, he is good, I thought to myself, listening to their conversation and wishing I could act like that.

"Well," Kelly started, "I was just wondering . . . you know . . . why you kissed my mom's arm yesterday," she said.

Graham's face went white, and he stood there with his mouth wide open.

"Graham, Kelly—you're on," came a loud whisper from behind. It was Mrs. Barker. Kelly hurried onstage, but Graham just stood there like a statue of the young Ebenezer Scrooge.

"Hurry, Graham," Mrs. Barker said again, this time pushing Graham onto the stage.

Kelly began her lines about how she wants to marry Ebenezer, but that she can't wait for him forever. Then Graham was supposed to say his lines about how important his work is and how he needs to earn money before he can settle down and get married. But Graham just looked confused. Mrs. Barker stood offstage whispering his lines to him from the side, but Graham looked like he didn't even realize he was onstage. Finally he began to speak.

"Your mom's arm?" he said, looking confused.

"Um, yes, Ebenezer," Kelly said. Then, trying to bring Graham back into the play, she grabbed him by the shoulders and said her lines again. "Look, Ebenezer," she said. "I can't wait for you forever." This time she said it loudly right in Graham's face.

Suddenly he shook his head and realized where he was. He looked out at the audience and stumbled through his lines. He made a few mistakes, and I think he added a word or two, but he made it through the scene. I wanted to talk to him afterwards, but Mrs. Barker grabbed me and told me to start looking for Tiny Tim's crutch, which was missing.

I finally found the crutch and lined up for my scene. Everything was going so fast. Before we knew it, the curtain had closed and Mrs. Barker was pushing us onto the stage. David was bringing out the Cratchits' kitchen table, and someone else carried out a chair. Within seconds, the Cratchit home was created onstage and the curtain was opening.

Sweat was forming on my forehead. I felt like the whole audience could hear my heart pounding. Each word spoken by Tiny Tim and the others brought my "plum pudding" line closer.

Then my moment came. My line. My one line. My "plum pudding" line. I put on my best "I love plum pudding" face, looked around at my pretend Cratchit family, and got ready to humiliate myself in front of every kid's parents in the school, when all of a sudden a siren sounded. It was so loud we all held our ears. It was the fire alarm. I looked over to the side of the stage and saw David pointing to the fire alarm on the wall and explaining something to Mrs. Barker. He must have accidentally set it off.

Mrs. Barker quickly went to the microphone and told the parents not to worry, that it was a false alarm and it would be turned off momentarily.

With all of the confusion, I still hadn't said my line. So, with the alarm blaring, I thought, *This is my chance.* Looking out at the audience, who couldn't hear me over the noise, I proudly stated, *"AND MOTHER MADE A PLUM PUDDING, TOO!"*

And just as I finished, the alarm turned off.

I did it! I thought to myself. What luck! I could have hugged David at that moment for saving my life. Of course I didn't, because he would have punched me. But the point was I was able to say my line without any humiliation at all.

It was perfect. At least it would have been perfect had Mrs. Barker not closed the curtain and told the audience that we would be starting the scene over again due to the interruption.

So all of us Cratchit children got back into our places and started over. This time I was not nervous. I was just *mad*! Nothing was going right today, and at this point, I didn't care. I was ready to be laughed at. *Bring it on,* I said to myself.

Finally, as Tiny Tim finished his line, I again opened my mouth and declared, "And Mother made a plum pudding, too!" Then I waited for the laughter. And as I expected, I heard some chuckles from the audience. Not many, just a few. I actually think one of them was my grandpa. And of course, there was a bunch of chuckling backstage.

Lights, Camera, Action!

As I stood there in my embarrassment, I noticed that we were already about three lines past my part. The chuckles were over, the play was continuing, and my humiliation seemed to have come and gone. Within no time at all, the curtain was closed. The next scene was being pushed onto the stage, and the Cratchit kitchen disappeared. Plum pudding was gone and would not return for another year, when some other poor soul who thinks he's going to be Scrooge gets stuck with the part of Peter.

It seemed strange that the reason for all of the worrying, faking sick, kissing Lizzy, and humiliation at play practice was over in a matter of a few seconds.

The rest of the play went smoothly, and we all came out and bowed for the audience. It felt good to hear all of the applause. I wanted it to go on longer. My eyes met Heidi's, and she smiled back at me. Hopefully, she still wanted that good-luck kiss.

Our parents came up to the stage and took some more pictures. I told my mom I had to get my coat and I would meet her out at the car.

Backstage, everyone was congratulating each other. I tapped Heidi on the shoulder and told her she did a great job.

"Thanks, Raymond," she replied. "How about that kiss for good luck? I know the play's over, but maybe it will help me get more Christmas presents." She smiled and, like before the play, took a step toward me. And again, just like earlier, I started to feel dizzy. Only this time my stomach felt queasy, too. Then my nose started to tickle. And as I was about to make my move . . . *"Ah-ah-ACHOOOO!"* I sneezed. And not just a regular sneeze but one of those huge sneezes that you need a tissue or two to clean up after. I guess I had caught Lizzy's cold after all.

Heidi jumped back. "Oooh, *gross!*" she said, staring at my messy nose. "You know, Raymond, maybe I'll take that good luck some other time. I don't want to get sick. Have a merry Christmas." Then she smiled and walked away. I watched her, thinking maybe she would turn around. But she just kept walking until she disappeared around the corner. Still, I stood there looking at that corner, wondering if she would come back. She didn't. *Maybe I should give up on this kissing thing for a few years,* I thought to myself as I wiped my nose on my sleeve.

Just then I felt a hand on my shoulder. It was Graham. "Sorry, *hermano,* I heard the whole thing. What a night," he said, shaking his head back and forth. "Hey, why didn't you tell me I kissed Kelly's mom's arm yesterday?"

"Sorry, I just couldn't," I said. "Not after seeing you skipping down the hall all happy and crazy like that. Let's just get out of here."

We walked out the front doors and down the stairs in our costumes, feeling sorry for ourselves. "Hey, Graham," I finally said, "do you remember Gordon Armstrong?"

"Of course I remember Gordon," Graham answered. I could tell he didn't want to talk about it.

"Well, it just seems like our fourth-grade year isn't going the way it's supposed to," I said. "We're not even close to being as big as Gordon was, I had to be the 'plum pudding' guy instead of Scrooge, you kissed Kelly's mom's arm, I kissed Lizzy . . . I could go on and on. I just thought this year would start out different. I thought we'd be more like . . . well, like Gordon Armstrong right from the start. Remember those first-graders we saw the first day of school? They didn't step aside when we passed by, like we did for Gordon. They just called us names and kicked me in the shin."

"Yeah, it doesn't seem right at all," Graham said.

Just then someone yelled from an open car window, "Bye, Graham—have a great Christmas!" It was Kelly waving at us, or at least at Graham.

We stopped and looked at each other. Graham's gloomy face quickly changed to a smile. As he was waving back to Kelly, we were interrupted again. This time it was a couple of first-grade kids. One of them pointed to me and said in an excited voice to his friend, "Hey that's the guy from the play!"

The other kid's face lit up. "Yeah, cool!" he replied. As we walked by, Graham looked at me with a big smile and said, "Go for it, *hermano*."

I looked at the kids, nodded my head, and said, "Hi, boys." Immediately, they stepped aside. We could feel their eyes still watching us as we walked past them into the parking lot. Suddenly, I felt six inches taller. I felt like a fourth-grade man. We smiled all the way to our parents.

Sure, this year hadn't gone as we'd planned so far, but Graham and I still had a lot ahead of us. Christmas was just around the corner, which is always a good thing. There was baseball season in the spring, and there was still half a year left to rule the school. Graham still had hopes for Kelly liking him, and Heidi would still need good luck somewhere, sometime soon, I was sure. I just needed to get rid of this cold first.

"*Ahh . . . ahh-choo!* Ooh, gross. I need a Kleenex."